I0547150

Salt Rich
Leanne Dunic

Harbor Editions
Small Harbor Publishing

Salt Rich
Copyright © 2024 LEANNE DUNIC
All rights reserved.

Cover art by Marcus Jernberger, "Mackerel"
Cover design by Brianna Protesto
Book layout by Brianna Protesto
Small Harbor Executive Editor: Kristiane Weeks-Rogers
Small Harbor Director: Allison Blevins

SALT RICH
LEANNE DUNIC
ISBN 978-1-957248-37-0
Harbor Editions,
an imprint of Small Harbor Publishing

"Salt Rich" was published in *Three Hearts: An Anthology of Cephalopod Poetry* 2024

Salt Rich

Contents

Yugoslavia, 1956

The baby's coming. The friend discreetly shows where the boat and oars are stowed. Direction doesn't matter, just speed. Jail could be three months or three years. They follow ship paths, along with the sharks. Only coordinates known: somewhere on the wrinkled Adriatic.

Bari

The camp in Italy is cold and unsanitary, with little food.
It cramps as Hungary revolts. The last time he ran away from
home: the shovel only intended to push the donkey along but
the animal turned and its head made contact. Its body stilled.
Now, a baby is on the way. What other options does he have?
The official understands they don't want to be separated
and arranges for them to get married. They're told that
this official has never shown compassion for a refugee.
She wonders if her belly is visible.

Bound

His skills as a cook have them transferred from Italy to
Canada's west coast, to an island like they're used to. A short
time ago he walked forty-five minutes to school in Preko,
where he won a copy of *Call of the Wild* for his studiousness.
A prized possession. Now, they board a boat to Halifax.
Each is given $28 for meals for the five-day train ride to
Victoria. He sneaks out at stopovers to buy cheaper food
to save their allowance. Through their windows: villages,
animals, vastness, bodies of water. A new wild. The baby
sleeps in their arms the whole time.

Baby

The baby's so sick he nearly dies. After the hospital recovery, a bill they cannot pay. The administrator calls to discuss payment, offers a temporary position as a cook in the hospital. The next day, another call. A cook cut his hand and is unable to work—the job now steady, permanent. The administrator writes a letter on their behalf and the government pays 90% of their medical bill. New world, new luck.

Tide

In a tidepool, they found some small eels. The slippery, undulating bodies were difficult to grasp. She had with her a cardboard purse she got as part of a Woodward's promotion, but the bottom dissolved on the ride home. Eels on the floor of the bus.

Vancouver Island, 1982

He receives a call at the hospital kitchen. His first grandchild
has arrived. At the nursery, he knows the pursed-lip baby
is me.

Salt Rich

Nearby, a combat ship sank. Divers retrieved bags of flour smelling of fungus, tasting of sea. During the second world war, villagers evaporated brine in limestone hollows. Night fishermen held lanterns overboard to attract octopuses. Used their tridents. Ocean alive: sea cucumbers, urchins, squid, sea horses. Easy to get meat from limpets, sea snails. The slick inside of a fish—gut odour indelible on fingers. Salt lines the skin.

Beatles

Summer days, she and I cut flowers, assemble bouquets,
bring them to the roadside to sell. Veggies, too. Gather warm
eggs from roosts. A walk to the park. Collect hazelnuts with
the blue jays. Dig for clams at the beach. Her eyes are the
colour of the sea. She doesn't know how to talk to me about
the Beatles, but she understands that my love is true. She's
surprised they have a song called "Paperback Rajka." I tell her
it's not her name, but "Writer."

Summer

Every morning at the marina. Return with baby bathtubs full
of rock cod, snappers, lingcod, sole, salmon. AM radio speaks
of war in the homeland. Poppies go to seed alongside the
backyard smokehouse.

Nourish

She makes palačinke. Apple fritters too. Fries from dug potatoes, served with his homemade ketchup. Vegetable soup, savoury thick, celery seed. Red lettuce vinegared, too tart for young mouths. His pork roast, legendary. A salt shaker, a few grains of rice. Love is unmentionable. We talk of foods we crave, foods we grew for one another.

Garage

Tools. Buckets and jars. Vats for chicken feed. Rarely a car, but boots and rats. The cement is often wet—water spilled from keeping flowers fresh or rinsing blood from the hanging buck.

Precision

The cat leaves only the rabbit's intact, emerald gallbladder
in the grass. On another section of green, a dead grouse.
Wingspan looks like lungs, like maple seeds. Piles of plumes,
a foot pressed on each wing, a swift pull of spindled legs and
we have meat.

Ugljan

They returned once. Hand-tilled, rocky land. A carpet of pine needles. Sharp, wide mountain grass reaches past the knees. Hidden: rabbits, snakes. Above: sparrows, finches, hawks. Yellow butterflies by the cabbage. Shade of fig leaf. Wind blows through the needled branches and holed rocks. A highway connects islands. Friends are dead or elsewhere.

Hands

He's picky, hardly eats—too thin for his height. His lanky body accomplishes the unimaginable. Hands as big as my head hold a sparrow that hit the window. His lips give mouth-to-mouth. His hands tend to grapes in the greenhouse, to the row of his precious roses. How does he not fall over from the weight of those hands? How do they remain soft as his petals?

Juice

They grow apples, pears. Turn the press to extract juice so
sweet it needs an extra part water. They believe in juice and
morning coffee with three spoonfuls of sugar. She's had a
lifetime of migraines. *Please drink some water,* I beg. She refuses,
and he says he won't touch the stuff either. He takes wine
from his coddled grapes. These days, instead of the farm,
she tends to a gull on the porch, feeding it bread she keeps in
a cardboard box. Sparrows beak the crumbs. I cannot tell her
how bread crumbles avian bones. She speaks again. How the
eagle took one of the hens in the field and how she no longer
wants to live. Nothing has gotten better since their son died,
yet there are always chocolates on the table. Meanwhile, in the
kitchen, he dissolves brown sugar crystals in water, leaves the
nectar on the counter for his ants to feed. One crawls into the
plastic bag he uses to gift me lemon cake, and he ushers it out.
It's difficult not to step on his pets' crawling, plump bodies.
Another climbs inside his shirt sleeve, and he allows this.
She collects the trampled ones from the floor.

Rotary

Not designed for ten-digit phone numbers. Each one shutters
and clicks after a completed circle. She remembers when
it cost $12/minute to call Yugoslavia. When there was a
Yugoslavia. In a lifetime, the only Croatian I've retained:
slušati—listen. Now, her mind falters, forgets I lack her
language. The line crackles. She speaks her native tongue
and I listen, trying to learn through her loss.

Nose

The cat's nose is concave, red, open. Two slits, wet breaths. It's a tough kitty. If they spend money on its care, that'll take away from their kids' inheritance. Since their son's gone missing, she can't lift her arms but can still pull her shirt closed. She forgets the word for muscles. He searches for a piece of paper that names her condition. *I could live another eight years,* she says. *That would be expensive.* She fingers the fabric at her collarbone. *How you come into the world is how you leave it.*

Winter

What's there to do? Nothing grows, and when the sills are clean, they're clean. The hens don't eat as much in the cold. The summer was too windy and bad for bees, unable to find a foothold. No pollination, no fruit.

Stroke

He knows something is wrong, so he puts a thermometer under his tongue. Dad takes it out to see that it's broken and tells him. He takes it from Dad and puts it back into his mouth.

End

In the hospital, Dad holds his phone so that his father can see me, but the camera is damaged, and all I see is a hazy impression on my screen. My love pours over the internet to his ears. Goodbye, and thank you for this life. The next morning, I dream of him standing in their house, wearing clothes without holes, each garment a matching forest green. He's not the ninety pounds he was the day before. You look good, I tell him. He smiles, then walks down the stairs to the front door to meet what has come.

Forever

His sister's grief is compounded by her dementia. *You can't live forever,* she repeats. She weeps every time we talk. *You can't live forever.*

Home

Before, she listened to the cluck of her hens. Here, it's the even easier-to-listen-to rendition of "Against All Odds." Their framed wedding photo faces her bed. On the table is a cup of apple juice that she did not grow or extract. I hold the straw to her lips and she drinks it down in one unflinching sip. She fidgets with her blanket like she did with her sweater after her son disappeared. Her fingernails are painted—the first time. She holds my husband's hands and mine and gives each one a toothless kiss.

Wake

Truck to Port Renfrew with nets, hip waders, buckets, stove, frying pan, sleeping bag. We embark, offer ourselves up to the wave. Trap, troll, trawl. Pull in smelts for the family, for the cat. Stray blue nets make new nests. Watch shells tossed whole. Tides grind sand—so many lives. Liquid can be so heavy. Abusive. Sums of salt, stripped beech, kelp whips. Toss us around, keep us alive, just enough.

Acknowledgments

"Salt Rich" was published in *Three Hearts: An Anthology of Cephalopod Poetry* 2024

"Salt Rich," "Nourish," "Summer," "Garage," "Precision," and "Winter" were published in *Hungry Zine* 2023

"Juice" was a finalist for *Smokelong Quarterly's* Grand Micro Contest 2021

"Wake" was published in *Vice-Versa: A University of Hawaii E-zine* 2020

Much gratitude to Harbor Publishing,
Tom, Kathleen, Matea, Sierra, Ryan, and my family.

Leanne Dunic is the fiction editor at *Tahoma Literary Review,* a mentor at Simon Fraser University's *The Writer's Studio,* and the leader of the band The Deep Cove. Her most recent project is a book of lyric prose and photographs entitled, *Wet* (Talonbooks 2024). Leanne lives on the unceded and occupied Traditional Territories of the Musqueam, Squamish, and Tsleil-Waututh First Nations.

About Small Harbor Publishing

Small Harbor Publishing is a 501c3 nonprofit organization. Our goal is to publish unique and diverse voices. We are a feminist press, and we are committed to diversity and inclusion. We strive to bring new voices to a devoted and expanding readership.

Small Harbor Publishing began in 2018 with the first issue of *Harbor Review*. The magazine is an online space where poetry and art converse. *Harbor Review* quickly grew and now publishes reviews and runs multiple micro chapbook competitions, including the Washburn Prize and the Editor's Prize.

In July 2020, Small Harbor Publishing was officially incorporated and began Harbor Editions. Harbor Editions accepts submissions through a chapbook open reading period, a hybrid chapbook open reading period, the Marginalia Series, and the Laureate Prize.

In 2023, Harbor Anthologies began with a mission to promote texts that explore social justice issues and highlight marginalized writers.

If you would like to support Small Harbor Publishing, please visit our "About" page at smallharborpublishing.com/about.